The Christmas Cats

The Christmas Cats

By Nancy K. Wallace

Illustrated by Cathren Housley

PELICAN PUBLISHING COMPANY

GRETNA 2011

For my beautiful daughters, Mollie and Elizabeth,
and their sweet kitties who inspired this story!—N.K.W.

To my grandson, Jackson, whose smile is the star on my
Christmas tree and the light inside my heart. —C.H.

The word "Pelican" and the depiction of a pelican are
trademarks of Pelican Publishing Company, Inc., and are
registered in the U.S. Patent and Trademark Office.

Library of Congress Cataloging-in-Publication Data

Wallace, Nancy K.
  The Christmas cats / by Nancy K. Wallace ; illustrated by Cathren Housley.
      p. cm.
  Summary: Eagerly anticipating their annual Christmas party, two sisters
safely stash the eight family cats upstairs before the guests arrive, only to
have the cats escape and wreak havoc on the festivities.
    ISBN 978-1-58980-979-6 (hardcover : alk. paper)
[1. Stories in rhyme. 2. Cats—Fiction. 3. Parties—Fiction. 4. Christmas—
Fiction.] I. Housley, Cathren, ill. II. Title.
    PZ8.3.W1586Ch 2011
    [E]—dc22
                                            2011002912

Printed in Singapore
Published by Pelican Publishing Company, Inc.
1000 Burmaster Street, Gretna, Louisiana 70053

At the end of a lane, in a house trimmed with holly,
Lived Elizabeth Ann and her sister, Miss Mollie.
They had a fine parlor and a porch where they sat
And a simply delightful assortment of cats.

There was Darwin, the fluffy; Dexter, the tabby;
The calico, Ella; and Dorrie, the crabby;
Harry and Ron, two fluffy white balls;
Olivia, the villain; and Phoebe, the small.

The house smelled of Christmas; the cookies were
    baked;
Their mother made gingerbread, scones, and three
    cakes.
She sent invitations to girls that they knew,
"Please come to our party! We'll serve tea at two."

The tree had been trimmed, the candles were lighted,
But sadly the kitties had not been invited.
They were banished upstairs, to the bedroom
  with treats,
Some dry food and milk, and a large can of meat.

At a quarter to two, the kitties heard tires.
The first to arrive was sweet Abby Myers;
Next came Sue Smith and Rebecca Wright.
Three little ladies all dressed up in white.

The girls all exclaimed at the elegant tree,
The mantels, the stairway, all trimmed beautifully.
The table looked pretty with snowy white linen;
The napkins had chocolates tucked neatly within
them.

The scents from downstairs were warm and enticing.
The cats smelled the scones and white Christmas
    icing.
They watched at the keyhole; they pawed at the door.
They peeked through the cracks as they lay on the
    floor.

Below, the fire crackled and laughter arose,
The kitties were restless, refusing to doze.
They rumpled the covers; they danced on the floor;
A small paw reached up toward the latch on the
    door.

They jiggled and wiggled, they bounced and they
   bobbed,
They stood on hind legs, and they rattled the knob.
The latch shifted once; the cats heard it click.
When the door finally opened, they ran downstairs
   quick.

The children were eating by candles and firelight;
The tree was just perfect; the food was just right.
With talking and laughter, no one heard the paws
   coming;
Then into the room the kitties came running.

Phoebe pounced on the table and scattered the holly.
Dexter dived for a sandwich and crashed into Mollie.
Olivia leaped for the bright chandelier
And landed instead in Elizabeth's hair.

Then came meowing, screeching, and clatters,
As eight cats assaulted the dishes and platters.
They gobbled the sandwiches, salads, and treats—
Gingerbread, strawberries, cupcakes, and sweets.

Darwin finished a cookie, then sipped some sweet tea.
And settled at last on Miss Mollie's knee.
Olivia crawled on Elizabeth's shoulder,
Ella just purred, wanting someone to hold her.

Each cat found a girl to sleep on at last,
And quiet returned to the ruined repast.
"I'm terribly sorry," Mom said with a tear,
"This party's our last. We won't hold one
     next year."

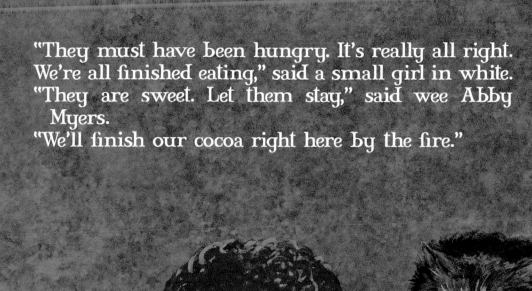

"They must have been hungry. It's really all right.
We're all finished eating," said a small girl in white.
"They are sweet. Let them stay," said wee Abby
  Myers.
"We'll finish our cocoa right here by the fire."

So the guests and the kitties retired to the fireside.
When Elizabeth Ann heard Susie confide,
"This party was fun! And I'll tell you that
The thing I liked best were your eight Christmas cats!"